I Was Waiting For A Sunrise In Nevada

Sunaina Verma

pencil

ISBN 978-93-5458-278-3
© Sunaina Verma 2021
Published in India 2021 by Pencil

A brand of

One Point Six Technologies Pvt. Ltd.
123, Building J2, Shram Seva Premises,
Wadala Truck Terminal, Wadala (E)
Mumbai 400037, Maharashtra, INDIA
E connect@thepencilapp.com
W www.thepencilapp.com

Author biography

She is a Dental Surgeon, a Fashion Model (Winner of numerous Beauty Pageants and represented her state Madhya Pradesh in National level Beauty and Talent Pageant), a Martial Artist, an Artist (Got her first painting showcased in an exhibition at the age of 16), a phenomenal Dancer, a Boxer, a sports person, a fitness enthusiast, she has finished numerous Marathons, a performer, a FOREVER LEARNER are the two words that best describe her and now the author of the Best Selling novel "Wholeheartedly- For A LifeTime".

From doing her own scientific researches or presenting scientific research papers and posters in International

Conferences to hosting chill Podcasts and having a fun YouTube Channel of her own, from being a zumba instructor to making her favorite italian dish.. she can make anything possible.

But I won't be wrong if I say that this is just 5% of who she is as a person, there is still an ocean of unexplored fields and a personality unleashed... Working hard, learning, falling apart and rising.

You can find her on social media by the following usernames:
Instagram, Twitter and Facebook - @isunainaverma
Youtube by SUNAINA VERMA
LinkedIn by Dr. Sunaina Verma
Podcast by "That NunChuck Girl Talks About…"

CONTENTS

Epigraph

"Is love keeping us alive
or
Are we keeping the emotion love alive"

-Sunaina Verma

Acknowledgements

For my family,
For my readers,
For all the love and support
This one is for you.

Sunrise-Sunset

I have heard it somewhere, 'We love someone and they don't, someone loves us but we don't'. This one simple and sweet line have so many emotions involved in it that doesn't even cross our mind the time when we read it but when we give it a closer thought then only we realise that the glance of someone walking inside the room.. suddenly giving you goosebumps, the feeling of someone smiling instantly giving you a smile and that feeling of 'Oh my God! What should I say next? I hope my hair doesn't look frizzy and it is nicely settled. I hope I'm not sounding stupid while talking to him/her' or that calm feeling of texting someone with all the chaos going on in your life and their one reply makes everything so calm and relaxing even if its just "I'm all good. What about you?". All of those feelings are nothing but cute, but what happens when the person you like doesn't have the same feelings for you? Or what if that one person whose smiling face makes your entire day doesn't care about your existence on this planet or even in the same room? Are you gonna feel the same or are you still gonna have those exact same feelings for that one person? Doing everything to keep them out of trouble even if it takes all of your time and energy and that makes you lose your time to complete your assignment or your important work is also fine for you because you don't want to see that one person face any problems and feel sad. Not even for a little time span. Maybe because seeing that one person sad.. Disheartens you.. Breaks you down completely. Their zero percent feelings for you doesn't change this.

But then there is that other person who is just another person for you, the person whom you never text, the person whose text messages you always ignore or you only text them when you are bored or you need some help from that person, who continuously asks you when and whether its a good time to talk or not but to you it's always a 'Sorry!! Some other time may be.' In short the person whom you simply take for granted, the person who according to you is just an idiot, a frustrated or just a desperate goofball TRYING TO GET YOUR ATTENTION but may be, just may be that idiot thinks about you all the time, or may be that idiot likes you in a manner that even this much of your ignorance is okay to that person, in the hope that someday you will give them a little, just a little bit time of yours being unaware of the fact that you don't even see their worth and adore someone else's presence in their life who in real doesn't even care about your crush. (If that's what you wanna call your one sided love for them because technically that person does crush your feelings. Right?)

Haha anyway...

The question here is that if someone asks you to choose between one of these two people. Whom will you choose? The one whom you like or the one who likes you?

I think you must have thought of choosing the one whom you like just because you like them and someday they will see that in your eyes and feel the same for you and then you will have your own heart warming fairy tale and may be some of you just thought practically and went with the other option and chose the one who likes you because of one simple reason that they liked you so much even when you didn't bothered about their existence.. So how much that person is going to care for you and love you now when they'll see and know that you chose them? Or above every other person in your life you chose them... they will obviously put all their efforts to keep you the happiest. But is it fair? Would that person have been your choice even if the person you like just shows up-to you after ignoring you and your existence previously, proposes to you and asks you to be their companion? Would that person still be your priority?

Now let's be a little honest with ourselves and accept that we would have dumped the other guy or girl at that very moment. Yes! It's dumb but that's what most of us would do, be a little selfish and idiot to put ourselves down and settle for what we want instead of what we deserve and ruin what we have in our faith.

Aloof this sounds pretty fine till here, right? No tears, no broken hearts, no broken bones, simply no drama, just some typical thoughts and some genuine reasoning on them. But these all things aren't this kind of sorted and simple in real life and it becomes more complicated and complex when you are in a professional field or science student as you have always been told that it's not a joke being in a professional college it requires your blood and sweat, you can never take it lightly, you will fail if you get distracted, you have to study for all the possible time after the 6-7hours of regular college, you shouldn't be spending your valuable time on social media which professional college students do really often (not all but most of them or at least the ones that I have met), it's not that they aren't serious about their future but having all these social media accounts are a trending thing or were at least cool then and following these trends and being really active on them makes everyone look cool so why not? And updating most of or all of our activities on it is cooler. And YES!! They don't actually take their studies that seriously until their exam dates are out and by 'they' I just mean my friends who are now in a professional college and I'm here in an engineering college trying to be a philosopher and understand about the feeling L.. O.. V.. E.. love.. I just want to know if it's some emotion that we made up to cover up our ill thoughts and actions or is it a genuine emotion even if it's for people who aren't our family.. Whom we met by chance in the path of our life. Anyways you'll know about me soon but for now let's get back to what I was telling you about.

The atmosphere of a professional college doesn't really have fun in it here to be honest, the breeze here has stress and a bit of smoke in the air, now don't ask what kind of smoke cause I won't be able to pen that down here. The sunrise usually gives us the hope of positivity and sincerity in our behaviour but the sunset takes it back as if that hope wasn't even there. Here people occasionally have seminars and conferences to attend and rarely get a chance to go on trips and vacations.. At Least most of them. And I'm saying this because I too have experienced all this being in an engineering college which was supposed to be a professional college but never really gave me any professional vibes. People do say that it's never about the place but it's rather about what's inside you but if it really didn't have anything to do with the place then why me and my friends were having all the similar experiences related to our college life. Maybe it's our age or maybe it had to do something with the idea of freedom that college life was supposed to give us but who knows?

You must be thinking 'why are we discussing this professional college atmosphere here?' so we are discussing this here because Aakriti is a student there. Yeah!! Aakriti is a second year student in a professional college pursuing dentistry. She is an amazing friend when it comes to discussing day to day troubles and concluding a solution for it. Not only girls but even her male friends reach her when it comes to any problem that gets a room in their head and makes them lose their mind or heart. She was the most sorted person that I have ever met. To her people were either important or didn't have an existence in her world. Her 'I don't give a damn attitude' was something that everyone hated but at the same time fell for that attitude hoping to be someone like that cause she wasn't giving a damn about whether you like her or not. She was everything that would make a girl go jealous of her and a boy to dream of her and what everyone thought was that she can have anyone that she wants but was that the reality? Was her appearance and confidence getting her everything that she wanted? Was all the attention easy for her to handle ? Was she even happy? Well!! This pretty fabulous girl happened to be my best friend but trust me she still happened to be a mystery to me. Always calm, always poise.. I never knew what's happening in her life and I never even bothered to ask because to me her life looked perfect. Because with that pretty toned face and those big green eyes it's even hard to think that she'll ever get stuck in some problem. Those eyes with a simple smile looked the way out to every problem and now when I'm stuck about the concept of love and the tsunami of emotions that one faces because of it.. I just wanted to know her story.. Hoping that she'll get me out of this pit just like she helps out everyone. So I reached out to her to know her story.. More like her love story.

But let me just flash some light on the fact that I know her so I know that this story won't be just about a pretty-ambitious girl her love life but it's also about a guy who fell for her without even knowing her and without even letting her know about his feelings and how things got twisted when they unknowingly and unwillingly alloweded their feelings to control their mind and actions. And I happened to know them both or at least I thought I do so I asked them to tell me their story but didn't told them that I'm getting in touch with both of them to know their sides of the story and how things went when I wasn't their cause I knew them both before they even knew each other and I still somehow have them in my life when I don't know if they are a part of each other's life or even each others thoughts.

So I reached out to her first and literally begged her to

spare some time from her busy routine and tell me about when and how she fell in love.. Well i obviously couldn't ask her all this directly cause its been really long that I haven't spoke to her or met her in person in years so I looked for her phone number from our friends group chat and called her and I just asked her to catch up with me sometime soon and she happened to be really excited about the plan cause she agreed and told me that we can meet each other the coming sunday at her place and she'll cook for us. She always happened to be this warm and welcoming so it felt like nothing had changed until I met her.

I reached her home and rang the doorbell.. I thought of bringing her some gifts but I didn't because there was no occasion and I was broke then. Don't judge me!! You are reading a novel, trying to figure out what love is and thinking of someone who doesn't love you or doesn't care about you being in their life or not being in their life. I can judge you too but I'm not doing that so shush your mind and let the judgements be... I'm just an engineer who was trying to be a philosopher and learn about all the emotions.. Avoid the thought of stability, I wasn't even earning peanuts.

Man!! She opened the door and I was stunned.. I was stunned by how beautifully and gorgeously she was aging. Sorry!! The use of the word aging is completely wrong here.. The way she looked, she was just getting prettier with every passing day. Her hair looked so smooth, not too long.. Not too short.. Bouncy.. Her skin was glowing the way water in a lake glows in the evening when the sun rays touch it. Her eyes were soothing like a calm lake with settled water and one single dark green lotus leaf in the center of it covered with the fencing darker than the night kajal as fencing so that no one falls in the depth of that lake. And then she pressed her lips in mere confusion that why I was standing there like a sculpture and smiled at me which made me notice her lips which now were covered with a bit of moisture of her mouth, it looked so soft and fragile and she had a lip shade of light brown color which embraced her lips on her face so well that made her look so perfect.

I kept on admiring her beauty while she was asking me if I'm fine and when I realized this after a min.. I complimented her that she looks prettier than ever. I went in.. She offered me a glass of water and then lunch.. She cooked white sauce pasta for us.. She used to live alone so it was easier for me to talk to her about anything. So after we were done with our lunch and some casual catch up talks and then I told her the reason for meeting her and how I want to know about her love life so that I can understand the emotion-love and get better in philosophy about the emotion that I never experienced.

She simply accepted it and chose to help me by telling her story.

The Ostensible Interaction

It was a usual day, yet a lot more annoying. I had asked all my friends to attend the conference the other day but it was on our vacation day so everyone was more like 'why do you even want to attend it? Let's just enjoy our day off and go to some cafe or have a bit of a party', but I don't know why I just refused those suggestions and yelled at them that 'fine! If you guys don't want to come so I won't even ask you guys to come and I'll go all alone but don't try to change my mind.' After that they all called me and even texted me but I wasn't in that level of anger where I would have calmed down and listened to any of them.

My phone was continuously ringing that evening but instead of answering any calls or checking the texts, I just setted an alarm for the next morning, muted my phone and kept it on the side table. It was 21:00, I had had my dinner earlier with mummy, she really cooks delicious food but I hardly appreciate directly, most of the times what I used to do was burp after finishing my dinner and when she used to look at me in disgust, I used to tell her 'Maa.. burps are obvious outcome of delicious food, don't look at me like that, it's not me who cooked this meal and laugh.' Mom and I had a friendly bond because of which I was able to discuss everything with her so I even told her about this conference and how much I wanted to attend it and also that none of my friends wanted to be a part of it and how they ditched me at the very last moment.

'I mean they shouldn't have agreed with the plan earlier.', I yelled in dejection.

'Look honey.. I'm really happy to know that you're taking your career this seriously already and trust me it's an amazing decision to attend the conference even without your friends and obviously you'll learn so many things about your field that way by not missing all these opportunity that you'll get but see it's your vacation time so there isn't anything wrong with not wanting to attend the conference because this time isn't something that you'll get in your daily routine so your friends aren't wrong either. They just have different priorities which is completely fine and as their friend you should accept the fact that none of you will have the same priorities every time and you have to accept it and respect their decisions because ultimately it's their life and it should be up to them what they want to choose.', She explained.

'But Maa, it's going to be a six hour long conference, that means I'll be there for six long hours and that means that I have to have my lunch there and none of my friends are coming.. I don't want to eat my lunch all alone in a crowd full of strangers Maa… I don't want people to stare at me with pity in their eyes.', I said in pure sadness.
Haha.. Dear when you start taking your career seriously, follow your heart and start doing what you consider is right or what according to your knowledge is best for you in a particular situation.. You will ultimately find yourself

standing alone many times and to be honest it'll make you aware with how this world is and how selfish people are in here and I hate to break this fact to you that in such situations you are going to find yourself all alone almostly every single time and if not every single time then most of the times but that doesn't mean that you are wrong or the path that you are choosing is wrong.. Sometimes people take the road that is less traveled and I personally feel that that's a very strong and bold step and sometimes people apart from that person who is taking that less traveled path.. Consider them foolish and dumb but that doesn't mean that they are wrong. People have their own perspectives and perspectives of people don't always go hand in hand. Let me break this into a simpler example for you.. Consider that you are in a park full of wealthy people around you and it's freezing out there but then you see a man who is just in a sheer shirt then what do you think people in that park are gonna think about him?', Mumma asked while explaining her point.

'I don't know.. Umm.. I guess some people are gonna think that maybe he is Fashion Conscious person and some are gonna think he tore his jacket somehow and dumped it somewhere or may be some are gonna think that he is wearing some extra layers beneath... and being judgy some might think that he is not capable enough to buy himself a jacket.', I tried to figure out some perspectives.

'Yes.. exactly my point, people think according to the capability of their thoughts and in the kind of situation in which their mind grew up.. So everyone has their own and unique perspectives. Also people have priorities.. Some consider their time valuable and spend it wisely but some spend it on things that aren't gonna help them grow as a person or in their career at all.. And sweetheart, the people who are going to discuss you standing alone in a crowd are the second kind of people.. So do you think you should let that idea of people discussing or gossiping about you bother you? Are you really gonna be the second type of person on your own and let this overthinking affect a day of your life that you haven't even lived yet?', she asked.

'Wow maa that was deep.. I never thought this way..', I said and hugged her tight.. Asking her how she always makes it so easy to make a decision?

She laughed a bit and said 'Experience honey!! Experience.'

After that we finished our food and I went to bed thinking how well my mum handles tough situations and how gracefully she even manages me and my thoughts that drive me crazy.. Wishing to be a bit more like her every single day leaving my own vulnerable and immature self behind.. After that I talked to dad over the phone as he was out of town for his work this month. So yeah!! That's all the people I have in my life.. Maa, papa and my few annoying-idiot friends.

***

'Seriously Aakriti!! I must say that you have a really sorted

20

life. I mean you have friends who drive you crazy at first but then put all their efforts to make you smile and you can discuss anything with your mom just like a friend.'

'Hahaha.. Yes!!'

'But is this it? I mean are they all the only people you have in your life?'

'Yeah Nishi!! That includes everyone.'

'No.. I mean there must be someone you forgot to mention about?'

'Nishu you don't have to do this you see, stop running around the bush, we have known each other since very long so you can ask me things straight.'

'Hehe yeah… I was just a bit conscious to ask you about your personal life directly.'

'We are talking about my personal life here… What's making you conscious c'mon?'

'I actually mean to say that you haven't mentioned your boyfriend yet.'

'Yeah.. That I certainly didn't…'

'Yeah so go on.. Tell me about your partner.. Don't hide it.. I want a love interest in the story that'll help me understand the concept of love.'

'I'm not hiding anything, it's just I don't have any partner to tell you about until-unless you want to know about my lab partner.'

'Okay!! You mean to say you don't have a boyfriend?'

'Yes!! That's exactly what I mean.'

'So are you trying to say that you never dated someone or you have never been stalked by someone?'

'Well I never said that.'

'So go on, tell me about it.', I said furiously.

'Okay!! Okay!! Calm down.. I'm telling you.'

The Relationship Trend

Okay!! So this started back in the year 2014, I was in my final year of school and to be honest everything suddenly changed so swiftly and it was way too weird to digest. I'm talking about the class atmosphere here, all we used to do was study, study and some more studies and in some spare time a little bit of acceptance of our situation that no matter how much we adore John Abrahim from the movie force, we all are ultimately surrounded by geek looking batchmates but the thing was even if no one was that much into those geeky looks and how flattering girls in my class found John Abrahim yet the number of couples in my class were increasing every single day, as if love was seriously a thing mixed in the air apart from pollution or may be having a boyfriend or girlfriend was just another thing trending other than facebook and big touch screen smart phones then.

And at a leisurely pace, I was noticing that each one of my friends was getting into a relationship as if it was supposed to be an assignment and there was some deadline to have a boyfriend or else we won't be able to pass the class. What crap I mean seriously.. Whenever we used to hang out together they all spent all our time praising how amazing their boyfriends are or how romantic and cute their gestures are or what they bought them for their very first chat anniversary or the anniversary of the time when she accepted their friends request on facebook or the completion of the first week of their relationship anniversary. I mean anniversaries are supposed to be for the celebration of one year of something.. Not the completion of a month.. I mean that would be a monthsary… maybe that could be a thing in the next few years.. Who knows? but I'm very certain that anniversaries are not supposed to be celebrated for a month or definitely not for a week.

(and see people nowadays are celebrating monthsary..', she added and winked at me).

I actually never said this to anyone but all these stupid things sounded cute at times not the anniversary part but the part of one blushing whiletalking about their significant partners or how much they try to make the other person happy about something or how much they tried to keep their other one out of troubles of class and I hate to admit that all these things made me wonder, 'Why? Why don't I still have a person by my side to do all these things for me and give me those butterflies with those natural pink cheeks.' but I think I was just in love with the thought of being in love but not loving someone in real because soon after that seeing them fight and arguing over mere not getting the similar colored or contrasting pins for their tie or not doing their own homework because they wanted to have some fun with their friends and play in the ground or because they wanted to have a nap is silly and dumb and seeing all these drove me down to a conclusion that it's better to not be loved at all instead of being loved for a bit or by the wrong because the way it gets all ugly afterwards is something that I don't even want to put in words. Those tears, those mean comments, those taunts and continuously wanting to hurt the other person's sentiments in some manner.. Why? Weren't you in love at all? Cause I don't think that an emotion like love is something that ends in a day.

I guess seeing my friends crying all night to sleep and seeing them mad just cause they are hurt and the other person isn't even sad in their absence… Ughhh!! Wait.. I think I should rephrase it to 'seeing them mad because of the presence of their ex-partner in the same class room breathing.. Just breathing and sometimes being happy or smart or right with their answers to the questions which were asked to them by a faculty was really scary at times. I mean you always knew that those people were your classmates and no matter what happens between you two.. that's isn't something that is going to change until one of you fails to pass the class. So why so much anger now? No one had the answer to this but I think it's just that the air which was filled with love earlier was then replaced by the air of hatred.. maybe because the love birds that we had in our class were just growing with time and turning into ravens or phoenixs.

This session was not happening at all.. With all these love-hate games going on in our lives our board exams just knocked the door and accept it or not even if we are not involved in any sports match and are just being the audience. Still that game affects our energy and here my friends were the team players and I was the audience in that stadium.. I wasn't a part of this but I was involved in some manner.

And with all this drama going on in one's life this is very certain that the way the twelfth board exam date sheet came, none of us wanted to top or score the highest but all of us just wanted to pass those exams and never see each other's face or at least some of the faces. I think all of us wanted this only because no matter how brilliant or sincere one was, when the results came out we all scored average like sixty to seventy percent and to be honest I think this is a nice score.. I mean I have seen people act like 'Ohh!! 60-70%? You should have worked harder as a child but don't get disheartened there's always scope for scoring better.. You still have many exams ahead of you.' I mean scope for better? Worked harder? These aren't passing marks.. It's twice more than that and it definitely is good.

And what do these people have to do with my marks anyway? Or anyones marks? Do you even remember my birthdate or are you aware of what I crave to eat at 4:00 AM in the morning? I don't think so then why are you being so opinionated?

We all finally got over all this drama.. I mean the exam and this was the point where I met people who appeared real uncanny to me that time. So anyway it was the birthday of Krishu (short for Krishna). She was a good friend of every single person in the class, you know how some people are just so good with their nature that no-one can really hate them? Yeah! She was one of them. So she was a good friend of mine as well and it was her birthday party and that party was the only hope for some genuine enjoyment.

And to be honest, I wasn't excited for her birthday.. I was just excited for the party.

***

'Offo Aakriti.. Where is the boyfriend?', I said irritatedly.

'Haha.. The boyfriend. Hmm.'

'What hmm?? Say something.'

'Honey!! We are getting there but not to the boyfriend part.'

'Then?'

'To the other person part.'

'Other person part?'

'The stalker part maybe.'

'You mean you were seriously stalked by someone?'

'Stalking is offensive and this person never offended me to be honest but I guess someone who liked me in real life scared me with his feelings somehow.'

'Hmm so you mean to say that you had an admirer?'

'Yeah.. I think.. If that's what you want to call it.'

'Oh!! Man.. All these school talks just made me forget about the conference part that you were telling me about... What happened at the conference then? Did you go to attend the conference or did you just skip it because your friends were not accompanying you?'

'Nishu. Just decide. What do you want to know about first?'

'Ok!! About the conference for now. I want to know what your decision was after all the conversation that you had with aunty.. I mean the way she talked to you was so real and precise that you obviously would have gone to the conference but how did it go then? Did you meet someone there? Tell me…..'

'Okay!! Okay!! Calm down.. I'm telling you.'

***

The Conference

After talking to maa, things were quite clear in my head. I had a confident state of mind to attend the conference the other day so I just arranged the things that I'll be needing in the morning to get ready for the conference, and went straight to the bed.

I was excited, it was the first conference that I was going to attend. I wasn't able to think about anything but the conference and imagining about the scenarios and the atmosphere of that auditorium, And I didn't realize but it was 3:00a.m. at night. I couldn't believe that I was so lost thinking about tomorrow that I just forgot to sleep. I went on saying, you have to wake up early tomorrow, stop thinking about all this stuff, just sleep, sleep, sleep, uhh! Stop talking to yourself and sleep Aakriti.

So the alarm clock rang, I woke up, got ready, had my breakfast with my mom, I just can't forget how delicious her breakfast sandwiches tasted that morning, simple yet delicious with not to forget a hot cup of coffee I just talked to her, told her that I made my mind to attend all the seminars/ conferences which are good for my career. She was happy with my decision being this practical. I then finished all my breakfast and drove off to my college. And it was so obvious that I was still only imagining how it would be? How I'll be interacting with people there because obviously I didn't wanted to sound childish to those people who would soon be my colleagues.

I reached the location at time, or I better say earlier than the time when I was supposed to be there, I was there outside the auditorium in the parking lot at 9:40a.m... I wasn't a freak but the conference was scheduled at 10:00a.m. so I was twenty minutes early and I didn't want to be there at 9:45am, so I was just waiting for the clock to hit 9:50 so that I'll get in the auditorium at 10 exact or may be five minutes earlier so that I won't be there with all the strangers around waiting for the conference to start. I was just trying to avoid any awkward moment. So instead assuming me a freak, you can consider it as a precaution.

It was 9:49 now, I was heading towards the entrance gate. The volunteer at the gate knew me, so he didn't ask me for any id or any entrance ticket and he simply searched for my name in his list, picked my entrance card and gave it to me. The auditorium was literally filled with a lot of people yet there wasn't any noise the way our school/college events used to have. I guess this is what people call professional meets and the professional event atmosphere. There was just one seat left in the fourth row at the side of the stairs so I rushed to it before anyone else occupied it. So I was on the seat that I wanted, I don't know why but I like the last benches while attending the regular classes and in such events I just love to grab a seat in the first few rows. The conference still had some time to get started. The guy sitting next to me passed me a pleasant smile and I didn't wanted to be the attitudy bitch so I just passed him a fake smile and looked straight to the stage and thankfully he didn't tried to talk after that so I was pretty satisfied that I just smiled back at him and didn't reacted in any uncanny manner.

~

It was now 11:30am. I must say it was a nice and very knowledgeable conference. The discussions were pretty fascinating about how implants can play such an amazing role and about all the materials that were used for implants. And it was a wow knowledge to me coz I just started my second year so was already fascinated by how a titanium post is surgically positioned into the jawbone beneath the gum line so yeah, it was an amazing decision to visit this conference.

Wait. What? No.

This can't be happening. Someone check the list please. What was a final year student doing on stage? How can he be presenting anything in such a huge conference? I mean he is just a final year student, all faculties are here, so many students are also here for the conference from all over the State. He can't be on stage representing anything. Someone please get him off the stage.

SOMEONE? OK PLEASE ANYONE?, I was shouting, ok wasn't actually shouting but things were getting messed up in my head. Yes, I was still right there sitting on the corner seat of the fourth row in a very calm manner (according to me) but I don't know what expressions I had on my face after seeing him. I think it was just a fierce reaction for his first glance, but I was genuinely calm now. And he was still on stage presenting his part of the conference. I always knew he was actually very capable of representing any topic (he, no doubt loved his professional field) and he was also very good in academics. I was actually now happy to see him there, he was handling it so well. I was feeling proud that he was there doing something that he was so determined about and somewhere in some corner of my heart, I was happy for him, I was happy to see him. It felt like I hadn't seen him in a decade and the concentration that I had in the conference suddenly got vanished, suddenly I was not able to feel my surroundings, suddenly I was just lost, lost in noticing how much he has changed or maybe he wasn't changed but he was dressed this way for the conference, obviously those big nerdy glasses that he used to wear were changed to a simple no frame rectangle glasses, he was looking so different from his usual look, actually he was looking nice; still nerdy yet nice.

He had the innocence of a kid on his face, formally dressed in a white shirt with a neatly tied black tie, black trousers, unbuttoned black formal jacket or blazer I don't know what to it is called, a coat may be I just don't know but that black jacket over his shirt and black formal shoes. He was looking so cute without having a beard on. Although he wasn't a great looking or a popular kind of guy, he was a simple and casual kind of person and he knew that very well. He was Avik, the guy who changed me a lot. I wasn't the person what I'm today, my thoughts about relationships were not complicated then. The way they are today, that time it was as simple as finding an object in "Dora, the explorer" (if you are more than 10years of age). I mean if you like someone you should tell them straight and if they feel the same, you guys should move forward in a relationship and if it's not then you can concentrate on your life, studies, simply on all the usual basic things instead of thinking whether he/she likes you or not, whether he/she is available or not, why is he/she smiling so much (while talking to the opposite gender) and all this drama. It was like if you want to be with someone today, you don't have to dig into their past or wonder about their future, cause what if there's no tomorrow. But he changed the way I think, or maybe he just completely changed me today. What I feel for a relationship is that it should be for forever not till you are not bored.

***

'So you're saying that this senior guy is the guy whom you dated? He was your boyfriend?' I asked in excitement.

'Uhhh, I don't remember saying any such thing?' Aakriti said with a mere awkwardness on her face. But the way you are telling me about him, I mean Avik, it doesn't appear like he was just a random guy, I said hesitatingly.

'Yes. He wasn't a random guy, I mean yes he was a random guy to me when I met him for the first time and really weird as well but then things got changed with time.'

Aakriti said with a peaceful smile on her face.

'Your smile is not making things clear to me Akku, at once you are saying things got changed and then this smile on your face, it's confusing me.' I said.

'Yeah, I was changed but this change was something that I really felt good about, you know when you know that you are mature but then things happen which make you think and then you realize that that was a kiddish feeling but then you actually see things like a mature person.' Aakriti said.

'Yeah, sure miss typically-typical mature adult. I said, rolling my eyes.'

'Hahaha.. Aakriti smiled wide.'

'So, where this conference lead? Were you still lost wondering how much Avik has changed in his appearance or you finally started concentrating in the lectures of that conference.' I said.

'Actually it was quite hard to concentrate on the further conference as there wasn't any, his presentation was the last second one and after that actually every person was distracted as it had already been four hours of all the presentations.' Aakriti said.

'Then what happened?' asked.

***

The Conference II

I didn't realize that I was so lost in the cold winds of the past that I didn't even hear a single word of what he said on the stage except for the last which was 'Thank you', but I was capable enough to sneak a peek at the notes that the guy sitting besides me was making, it was 'Advanced imaging in Dentistry and he also wrote something related to that only but i simply wasn't interested to know about what it was at that moment. I just wanted that event to end and get out of that place.

Being there having no interest left in the event anymore just made everything annoying. I was just looking at all the people on the stage with a single thought that guys please get a better dressing sense, such nerds. I was doing everything to get rid of what i had in my mind previously, so just when I got bored judging the outfits of the people on stage, I was randomly looking here and there as using phone would have made any faculty go mad at me if in case they encountered me doing that so i guess wandering eyes for something to get my mind engaged in was a better option than doodling on any page in my copy (wasting paper) or using my phone. And then those two wandering eyes of mine finally got something, Avik was looking at me, that was the time when we shared an eye contact, our first eye contact. He instantly passed a smile. He was standing at the side of the stairs of the stage, it was the side area, I forced a smile on my face as I didn't wanted to appear rude and then he waved at me and raised his eyebrows in a manner to ask me about how's everything, I just nodded as I had to respond but I still had that smile on my face and then I looked at the stage just to avoid the situation or any further exchange of expressions.

Thankfully it was the last presentation of the event, whatever that presentie on stage was saying was more like this blah-blah, that blah-blah and what not blah-blah not coz he was not presenting well but cause I was just waiting for the time to get out of the auditorium and the time he said 'Thank you for being such patient listeners', I just grabbed my bag and the notebook in which I was making notes (at least the one in which I thought of making notes) and started walking towards the entrance from which I entered as it was now the exit. But the crowd wasn't making this happen, the time the conference ended was like a flood of people and way more worse than a water flood, elbows hitting you, people randomly going here and there, it was terrible. But anything which was keeping me away from Avik at that time was okay to me.

I somehow managed to get out of that auditorium and the time I got out.. I just breathed in relief that finally I'm out of it and I don't have to face Avik, so I put my notebook in my bag that I had in my hand all the way while coming out and that was the time when I bumped into Avik.

'Hey!! Rushing somewhere?' Avik asked with a grin on his face.

'Not really but kind of,' I somehow managed to speak.

'If it is not really real then why don't you accompany me for a sandwich? I'm really famished, I mean I would have eaten that mic on stage.'

'Out of nervousness?'

'Not out of nervousness, uhh.. I mean fine I was a little bit of nervous but moreover I was hungry, I worked on my ppt till late and then couldn't get up even by my ringing alarm. I'm telling you about these gadgets. These stupid gadgets are seriously of no use.'

'Yeah sure but anyways you seriously mean that you are here with you're here with your tummy all empty?'

'Yeah. You can say that but I saw you rushing somewhere so it's fine if you don't have the time to join this human who has been without food since this long and can faint at any instance.'

'Uhh.. You better not use that puppy face with such dramatic lines for company.'

'So?? Is that a yes?'

'You can get faint here so you better start moving.. your sandwich won't fall from the sky.'

'You know I'm your senior right. You are not supposed to

talk to me this way he said with a grin on his face in a teasing way.'

'Mr. Avik Shah, do you want company or not?'

'Yes.. Yes.. C' mon be a sport. It was merely a joke.'

'Yeah!! fine.'

'Okay then miss Rai before you change your mood let's just go get my tum-tum some yum-yum.'

'Hahaha... You and your jokes.'

We both were smiling and then left for the sandwich bar that we had near our college. For a moment I just forgot that we ever stopped talking or how miserable yet amazed I was when I saw him on the stage. It wasn't even like a senior-junior formal thing, it was a friendly vibe. A vibe that just makes you happy for no apparent reason.

The cafe wasn't really far so we decided to walk there, the walk was calm, the weather wasn't that cold anymore, it was near about 1:25am the sun was shining high sparking the hot rays and making everything nicer.

'I know you from our school days Akku..', I said with confidence.

'Yeah.. You do know me... so?'

'So I don't think I ever encountered a guy named around

Avik.'

'Yeah I bet you didn't, so what?'

'You named this guy Avik, so are you trying to tell me that what you are telling me is merely fiction? I asked you to tell me about your relationship.. Your love story, your love life.'

'Hey!! Hey!! Calm down you little angry bird, don't you even dare to think about punching me in the face.'

'You know what.. I won't even think about it, I'll just do it right away and rush to grab her arm.'

'Hey!! Watch it you mad psychopathic bitch, don't even try to get close to me. At least listen to me first.'

'WHAT? You weird ass chick, you ruined my whole time, I thought you would tell me everything honestly 'Ms Nishi Yadav, let me get this clear to you that I haven't lied about anything, what so ever I said is real but you.. Ugh.. Just making things up.'

'Nope, what I have done is that I just changed some names and the locations. Nothing else. Okay? So you better not call me a weird ass chick.'

'That's so not fair, you changed the names in your story and you didn't even bother to tell me for once?'

'Obvio, I thought you wanted to know the story, nothing

to gossip about.'

'Yeah but I feel cheated. Are you getting it? Really CHEATED.'

'You know what? It is gonna be this way only. So decide whether you want the plant or you wanna leave it for some flowers?'

'Huh.. I can't believe I'm agreeing with you on this plant and flower thing but okay. You have the right to manipulate the names here.'

'Haha.. I never felt this powerful before.'

'Okay!! Now fathom my situation a bit as well and get back to your story it's 5:45 p.m. and I have to get back to my place at 7.'

'Oh yeah!! We didn't realize the time at all, let's get to the kitchen, ll make you some coffee.'

'Yeah please, running after you to punch your face really exhausted me today.'

We went to Aakriti's kitchen, it was really clean (being someone who stayed in hostel in the last 6years of her life, I had to appreciate how clean and managed everything at her place was, even though she was living there all alone but she managed it like a lady not a college student).

Aakriti's phone rang..

'Nishu can you just check if it's Mumma's call and if it isn't then just put it on silent.', she requested.

'Ohk I'll just check but you better make the coffee nice, just said in a teasing way and she smiled like a child saying I won't let you complain about the coffee.', I said in a fun manner.

I checked her phone, it showed AARUSH CALLING, I replied to her 'Naah, this isn't your mom calling, bas kol aashiq lagte hai aapke (must be some admirer of yours), haha don't start it again Nish' she said and got engaged in coffee preparations. That name Aarush suddenly reminded me of someone so I decided to check her phone for a confirmation (the phone was kept on the table in the kitchen and wasn't protected at all so it was easy to sneak out the caller details). And these days it's not hard to get the details of a person, you just have to go to the messaging apps and check out their display picture alias dp and that's it this guy was no other than my school best friend who wasn't in my contact anymore, he didn't even texted me even once after school and here he was calling her. He is a bloody piece of shit. I could have killed him and would have done it literally at the time I recognized him as my friend from school who always used to drive me crazy by his unstoppable chatterbox individuality who never knew Aakriti in my knowledge.

You know the best thing about being raised in the same locality is even if you stop talking to each other, you know what the other person is doing. And here I was so mad at him that I wanted to kill him at this moment.

Before getting out of there I thought that it would be a good idea to just go through some of their previous whatsapp messages. And then I realized this idiot old friend of mine was so much into this pretty bimbo who liked someone else like crazy at some point or maybe at this moment as well but first I had to be sure about Aarush's feelings so I just thought of an excuse and left Aakriti's place after the coffee, telling her that I'll be back tomorrow for knowing the rest of the story.

***

The Forceful Encounter

I was so fiercely impatient to know everything that was happening between these two friends of mine. I went straight to Aarush's home and knocked. His mom opened the door.

'Nishi? Hi beta, is everything alright? You have been knocking on the door as if you had made up your mind to break it.', His mother said in a worried manner.

'I'm sorry aunty, I didn't realize that it was that bad so I apologized to his mother.'

'It's okay beta, I'm glad to see you, you are here after a long time. Where were you all these days?', Aarush's mom asked after inviting me inside of her house. (She is polite enough to invite me even after I nearly broke her door.)

'I was just busy in the hurdles of my college life aunty and got some time off today so I thought it would be pretty cool to visit all the school time friends.'

'That's really thoughtful of you, wait I'll get Aarush informed that you are here. I bet he will be really surprised to see you here.'

'Okay aunty.' I simply replied trying to hide all the thoughts running in my head.

[Aarush Entered]

'What the hell. Nishi? Man you completely are giving me a shock by getting here at this time that too after so long.' He said, trying to show off a bit of his sarcasm and care.

'Dude!! We so really need to talk.'

'What?? Don't tell me that you are here to break up with me. Please don't leave me Nishi. What will I do without you? Please don't.'

'Will you please stop this rubbish and listen to me?' I said fiercely.

'Okay man.. What's wrong? What are you so furious about?'

'Do you have someone in your life?'

'Yeah.. I have a lot of people in my life. You know. My family, friends.. You..'

'No. Not like that. I mean like a partner, a genuine partner.'

'What? You mean a gf?'

'Yeah!! Do you have any?'

'Yeah!! You are my gf.'

'Please be serious and give me an answer.'

'No. I don't.'

'Then tell me if you have feelings for someone? Genuine feelings.'

'What kind of question is it yaar?'

'Just answer... Yes or no?'

'Yes. Will you now tell me what's up in your head? You are scaring me now.'

'Oh nothing!! I'm just trying to know how people feel for someone when they like them, how badly they want them and how much they think about that person whom they like. You know, it's just a research about human behavior. So I thought to know these things from a guy's perspective and my old school friend will be perfect for this (didn't wanted to embarrass him by letting him know that I know Aakriti and I have read his texts in her phone so I just thought that this will be a better way to know all this.'

'Will you please help me for the sake of our old and still so fresh friendship and remembering that I always saved your ass from all the punishments in our school days.'

'Is it like a tic tac toe thing? You marked the O so I have to mark the X.'

'Yes it is. Now please don't say no, I requested him, making a puppy face which I knew he won't be able to refuse.'

'Okay fine.', he said.

Aarush was always a light hearted person, he wasn't one of those six pack ab guys but he was a gentleman kind of human. I guess that's why it was so easy to get him to agree to this thought of sharing all his feelings that he had for Aakriti.

He was the kind of person who never took relationships for granted or just for some showoff purpose, I guess this was the main reason that I was so excited to know his part of the story. The part about how he met her and what he exactly had in his heart for her.

The First Sight

'It was a regular day, the sun was shining, the birds were twittering and I was asleep continuously snoozing my alarm that morning because like usual days I was awake till late and I was watching horror movies.. eating chips and drinking soda. Even if I wasn't and I still am not a morning person so yeah it's just an excuse to not to appear too lazy and me being the most pampered person in my family, I was never disturbed or called the lazy one but that morning mum kicked my butt to wake me up. I was shocked and a bit confused about what was happening and why she kicked me. Actually she didn't really kick my butt but you see it was 8:30 in the morning and I wasn't used to getting this kind of treatment so I simply asked.. actually kind of complained to my mom that 'Maa.. It's so early in the morning, I don't have any exams or school today. I completed my higher secondary a few months back. Remember? Why are you waking me up now?'

'It's your counselling today. Don't you wanna join college?', Maa said irritatedly.

'What counselling maa?', I said, rubbing my eyes.

'The college allotment counselling of the university. Don't you remember you gave a competitive exam for this and now that you have scored good, you don't even remember it?", maa said with massive aggression in her eyes.. in a furious manner.'

The fact that she was screaming in mere anger and disappointment, I didn't want to accept that I forgot the counseling schedule completely so I instantly tried to cover up this silly mistake of mine by getting out of the bed first before I annoyed her more covering up the situation by saying "I do maa, I do remember it. I said and rushed to the washroom to get ready but most importantly I wasn't ready to handle the teacher's anger that my mom was about to explode on me at that moment. Seriously man, having a teacher as a parent is nice until it's not related to your education. Once it is they are the most strict parents that one can have.

So I left home after having some fried eggs with toast, and was there at the university at 10, yes I was late but the professor there in the hall just taunted me a bit and then let me in, as I interrupted him while he was making the students aware about the counseling procedures. I was a bit embarrassed and annoyed because of his taunts so I just went to the first bench that I found vacant and got seated. And the rest of the counseling was just formal and boring so won't talk about it. And just jump to the part where I fell, where I fell for her exactly when I saw her. You know boys like me don't just fall for anyone. Neither do we check out every girl around, the girls with artificially straightened hair, skinny jeans are our preference. You know what I mean right?

'Yeah the artificial bimbo's who hide behind a really thick layer of foundation Perfect choice.' Nishi said furrowing her eyebrows.

'C'mon don't be judgmental Nishu, I said we check such girls out but listen to the whole scenario first, Please!!' I requested her to stop assuming everything just because of a wrong statement of mine.

'Okay. Continue.', Nishu said with a straight face.

'Thank you!', I responded and continued with my side of the story.

So it wasn't like what said previously, she was in an Indian ethnic wear, a turquoise color kurta with a pair of jeans and simple fiat heels of may be two and a half inch and her hair were partially tied with a clutcher, I'm not sure but I think you girls call it half pony, and she was wearing a very decent shade of lipstick hiding the luscious red lips, and a eyeliner over it on those big eyelashes, that eyeliner was really enhancing her eyes. I think lipstick and a very thin eyeliner was all the makeup that she was wearing. Her hair was not straightened, I mean they were straight.. real straight not like those artificially flattened hairs, there were few curls in her hair as if she was used to of tieing them in some different patterns. No nail paints, no watch, no ring, nothing, simply no jewellery. Yet amazing.

'What?', Nishu said shockingly.

'What, what?', I questioned.

'Do you guys seriously check out girls with such keen observation?', she asked.

'No. I just looked at the girl from top to bottom in a glance and then looked somewhere else on the earth but I told you she was different, not my type but I was not able to take my eyes off her.'

'Wow man, I'm pretty impressed.'

'I told you, so next time have a little patience before getting such character assassination of someone in your mind as a result of their one mistake.'

'Yeah fine. I'm sorry.'

'Sorry? You have known me for such a long time and then you are assuming I am some sick kind of person. I'm disappointed, more than that I'm hurt.'

'Hey, I'm so sorry, I didn't know a few words can cause you so much trouble, Nishu said trying to convince me.'

'Hahaha. Look at your face, God!, I said trying to make fun of her.'

'You creep, I hate you..', she said, punching me on my bicep.

'Okay so continuing from where I was, she was amazing.'

'Yeah okay!! Amazing girl, you lost your mind, you fell in love at the very first sight when you saw her, what next?'

'What happened next is that she spoke to me but I was so lost in appreciating her beauty that I was not able to understand that she just spoke to me.'

'What she said?'

'Is there any more formality left after this?', passing a strange look.

'Sorry What?', I responded with a confused face.

'IS THERE ANY MORE FORMALITY LEFT REGARDING THE COUNSELING', she asked.

'No. No.. It's the last. We just have to handover all the original documents to them with our signature.', I responded, being formal.

And then her name was called and she left.

And yes!! This was the first interaction that I had with her.

'You call it interaction? Seriously? Are you kidding me Aarush?', I reacted furiously.

'Yes.. She talked to me and I talked to her so it was an obvious interaction.'

'Jesus Christ.. God!! Please put some brain in the head of

this boy.'

'Hahaha..', I laughed.

'What then? How did you manage to be such a person who can call her late at night?', I asked.

'When did I mention here that I call her late at night?', he asked impatiently.

'Umm.. Just the time when you were appreciating her beauty.' I said nervously.

'Nishi.. I know what I told you.', His anger was so clear that even the room was getting warmer every second and I was not able to lie to him anymore so I told him why I was there and how I came to know about Aakriti.
After confronting every bit of the truth I left his place. He was no longer in that temper but he was pretty disappointed that I didn't ask him what was in my mind straight.

The next day I went to Aakriti at her place to learn the remaining part of her story.

The Cold Vibes

Aakriti was making her breakfast and some coffee for me as well but today there was something in the room. Except for me and her there was stress, kind of anger and something like a volcano that can burst at any instance. I knew that Aarush must have told her about what happened but I wanted my story so I hesitatingly, breaking the silence, called her name. 'Aakriti?'

She was silent but anger was there on her face.

'Listen please', requesting, I asked her to hear my half of the story.

'Listen to what Nishi? That you checked my phone?'

'Look, last night you asked me to check who was calling and then after I saw his name on your screen, I was curious and then things lead to another and I'm really sorry for that.'

(I told her that Aarush has been a friend of mine for quite a long time and that my intentions were not to hurt anyone's sentiments. After listening to me, she was calm, accepted my apology and then we finally were there to continue with the rest of her part)

'So what is he to you? I mean Aarush. The way his feelings appear towards you, it's hard to digest that he hasn't proposed to you yet.'

'How much has he told you?'

'Till the part where you asked him something about the counseling procedure and left.'

'There is nothing more to it actually, I left and I got the admission in that college but I never joined as I got a better opportunity and even though social media was a trending thing that time but I didn't have an account on any such site that time and after months passed, I made an account on facebook and we somehow got in touch and he reminded me about everything that we talked a bit in the counselling, that's how we got in touch and yeah now we are pretty good friends.'

'So you are his friend and it's been quite long but are you? I mean do you? Uhh I don't know how to ask this.'

'If I'm not wrong, you are trying to ask me whether I'm aware of his feelings for me or not.'

'Yes. I mean that, I said with a grin on my face.'

'Yes!! I'm very well aware about his feelings for me as he himself confesses it to me every now and then.. actually whenever possible.'

'So? You must be aware of how crazy he is for you. Right? And you still want to restrict him to the friend zone Aakriti, Why?, more than anything I was shocked with her such response. Every girl dreams of a guy who loves her like crazy and he is that crazy for her but I guess she wanted him as a friend more than as a lover, companion or a partner.'

'Yes. He is an amazing guy, and I'm aware that what he has for me is something that not everyone gets from their companion or maybe that every second person desires this from their companion but what he has for me is something that I still have for Avik. And today I might accept him as a partner respecting what he has to offer me but I don't think that it will be fair to him. He will be there to care for me, protect me and also to support me in all the ups and downs that I face or that I will face in future. I'm very sure about it but would I be able to do the same? Would you ever feel the same for him? in simple words I CAN'T, what he has for me is something that I already have for someone else and no-one can change that fact and he being such a loving person and having pure feelings for me he won't give up on me ever and he doesn't deserves to get treated this way, in fact no-one deserves to get treated like someone as ordinary as the other people around by their partner.
Because love doesn't happen overnight?
And love at first sight isn't even a real thing?'

'But what if it is Aakriti? What if love does happen overnight. What if love at first sight is a real thing.'

'I respect him and I respect his feelings as well and my one YES can turn things into a relationship, maybe that is something that he wants and I'm very well aware about it but he doesn't deserve getting treated as someone ordinary. He deserves all the importance and care that one should get in a relationship and this is something that I can give him but I definitely can't feel what he feels for me and I don't want to cheat on him this way and hurt him every other moment.'

'After listening to her it was not the same, what she said was different, not something that one gets to listen to so usually. The people around this generation are more about fancy cars, showoff dresses and fake feelings that they can show off on their instagram accounts. I know this very well because I myself am a part of it but I guess she wasn't.'

After listening to her, I wanted to know what happened to her and Avik and her previous relationships as well. That if she is this deep and doesn't take relationships for granted then how come she had any in the past and how they lead to a break up.

So I insisted that she should tell me something about her previous relationships, about the people she had in her life before Avik and to continue it with where we left the part of Avik and her story.

The Reality Check

'See Nishi, the relationships I had in my school were mainly due to peer pressure and you gotta have one bf/gf to maintain your so-called style statement. And the time you are in school, you are not even sure about what love is or what relationships are meant in one's life, the importance, the passion, the love, you are aware about nothing.'

'Wow man, you really have a lot of depth as a person in the current situation, and I was so unaware of it all this while.'

'A wiser person once said, give your heart to the wrong person and see yourself doubting your worth for years.'

'Who said this?'

'Me', she said. Lighting the mood a bit.

'Yeah right..', I said 'Miss I'm great at everything, taunting her in a fun way.'

'Okay so continuing from where we were, I had some relationships before I met Avik and Avik was the person that thought would be calming the storms of my life and putting everything perfectly in the box at the right place and henceforth I confessed him about my feelings that I had for him, after a complete year of knowing him but his care was something may be that I took wrong or I don't know what but you see a guy should not be this much caring or protective for you if he is already seeing someone that too from past seven years or probably eight now. I knew this would hurt and this hurted as well and to be honest I checked his gf's facebook ID more than I ever checked or stalked his ID and I used to think like why her but not me?

I was at a point where I was comparing my features with hers, my face with hers, my hair with hers and everything that if I'm beautiful enough to catch everyone's attention then why I'm not getting the person that I want but I was just being foolish and disrespecting his love for her, I was also disrespecting her by judging her without even knowing her personally and most importantly I was disrespecting myself by comparing me and my uniqueness with someone else which isn't fair to my own self.

Avik had his heart taken but he might have something for me as well.. Call it his concern as a senior, call it care as one human to another human or anything but what's important is that he cared and I fell for him and he already had his girl, not by his side but in his heart she was with her and may be what they have is that strong enough that even after being in a long distance relationship they are still so strong.

And crying for someone who can never be mine is

something I don't think anyone should do because maybe if you are not getting it, that's what is written for you and maybe it's ruining your peace at this moment but that can be the best thing for you. I accept what I feel for Avik can't be changed and I don't even want to change it. May be someone, someday will come to my life and make me understand that 'Why it never worked with anyone else?' and that will be the best thing; when someone comes to your life and refuses to give up on you, denies to walk away in hard times or no matter how hard you are that person will look into your eyes and tell you that I know you are hard to be with but you have someone who can handle all your tantrums and that's me. And that day, you won't miss anyone from your past and that day will be a gifted present to you by your own self because you honey, refused to get treated for less and refused to treat someone else any lesser.

Or maybe he isn't at all like what I thought of him. Maybe he intentionally didn't tell me about his long relationship because he had some other intentions. Who knows? Cause you know falling in love with someone and staying in love with that same person is for strong souls that too without getting involved with someone else.

So yes! I had a crush on someone, I had relationships, I had my heart broken too but I never left living. I never stopped enjoying my life and most importantly I never stopped loving myself.

So Nishi this is my story, I had a guy whom I thought I loved and I have a guy who loves me to the extent that I can consider myself the luckiest person alive but sadly these two persons are not the same for me, I had all the sugar and spice to add but I prefered kedgeree.'

'Don't you ever feel like what would happen if someone of yours would never come? Will you regret refusing Aarush?, I curiously asked.'

'Yes! Maybe that SOMEONE will never come and maybe one day I'll regret refusing Aarush feelings for me but you know what? We are never aware of what would happen tomorrow and how things will change, and you know even if I regret about it in future, somewhere in my heart I'll be aware that that's what's right so that's okay.'

This was hurtful and to be honest, I couldn't see all this happening with Aarush that too because she isn't confident about her feelings. I had to tell Aarush about my feelings and the fact that he is the only reason I wanted to know about this feeling- 'love' and sort my emotions out, I can't let him get into this deep pit which will lead him nowhere.

I couldn't handle the fact that I was so afraid of confessing my feelings to him that I let him go away like this. I like Aakriti but this isn't right. She doesn't deserve him, I do and he deserves the same amount of love that he has to offer. He deserves that quality of love in his life, not some confused girl. With all these things in my mind I told Aakriti that I have to see Aarush right now and I just grabbed my stuff and I rushed to his house to let the volcano of my feelings burst.. Without even thinking that it might turn lives into ashes.

And before I could realize anything.. I was at his doorstep.. all in sweat, trying to catch my breath… I checked the time in my wrist watch. It was seven in the noon. Aarush opened the door for me asking if everything is fine and I hesitatingly said yes, adding that I want to talk to him about something really important. He let me in.. asking me if I wanted a glass of water or anything to eat and to keep it low because his mother is upstairs sleeping because of the heavy dose of medicines that she took because she had a headache.

I took a glass of water, sat on the sofa and asked him to sit beside me.

'Nishu? Is everything alright? You are scaring me every other day to just some different level.'

'No! Everything is not fine. I really need to speak to you about something and I want you to understand it nicely before reacting.'

'Okay!! Tell me what it is?'

'See Aarush.. You know Aakriti, you know why I went to see her after this long.', I said, assuming she might have told him everything by now.

'Yeah!! She mentioned once that you were keen to know about her concept of love or something like that only.'

'No. I just wanted to know how love makes you feel, how it changes you as a person if it changes you and I wanted to understand all that before confessing my feelings to you.'

'What feelings? Nishi? What are you talking about?'

'I need another glass of water', I said and went to the kitchen and he followed me there.

After sipping water a few times I told him about my feelings straight.

'See Aarush we have known each other for a really long time and I have always liked and protected you from all the problems which so ever I saw coming to you and I don't think that I would have done things like that for someone who is just a friend to me. I love you. I really do. I'm the one that you deserve to have in your life. I'm the one who deserves your love.. Not that girl who can't even think of anyone or anything apart from her own self. Let's just forget whatever you were doing. I'm not mad at you. You were just lost because I wasn't there for you that time.. By your side to take care of you and to protect you and that's how all this happened. I just distanced myself from you to be sure about my feelings and now that I'm here just tell me you love me and we'll make this world our own little fairytale and live happily ever after.. Just the way they show in movies.'

'What are you saying? Are you even in your senses?', he said, refusing all my feelings that I just explained to him.

'Yes!! I'm in my senses Aarush. I love you and I mean it.'

'Listen.. You are my friend, you'll always be and I respect your feelings for me.. Trust me I do.. But I don't feel the same for you and I think you should go back home now.. It's getting late.'

'Is that all you got to say? After everything that I just confessed to you. Is this how you are going to deal with this?' I asked, trying to control myself from shattering.

'See Nishi.. As I said I respect your feelings but I love Aakriti and I just don't feel the same for you. I never have. So I think it's better for this situation that you leave now.'

'You know what? I'm so much in love that I'm barely in my senses and my peace is much more important to me than your existence in my life so it's better for us that you leave now.' I said and before I could feel anything I was stabbing a knife in his back.. Again and again.

The tears on my face got my heart and me so numb that before I could realize I had his blood on my hands. I couldn't feel or understand anything. I was just stabbing him again and again. Asking him to leave me and let me be in peace and he was just screaming in pain. 'Nishi, what are you doing?' came a faint sound. It was aakriti she came and snatched him out from my hands the way she did it like before.

Then I heard Aarush say the worst thing.. He told Aakriti

that 'he wanted to wither in her arms then to bloom in this world.' with tears in his eyes. They were hugging each other while she was trying to stop his bleeding from the wounds. They were in front of my eyes. Those two together and I was right in front of them watching making promises that she won't let anything happen to him. These two left me all alone and now she was also alone, the reason for my condition. I won't let her get away with this, I couldn't let her get away with this. I had to end this right here before these two could hurt me anymore. I went walking to her slowly with the same knife with which I stabbed Aarush with the intention to do the same. I aimed my knife at her in the air. She was still trying to stop his bleeding waiting for the ambulance.. Putting all the necessary efforts to save him unaware that she is about to have a blood bath of her own blood. I aimed my knife, I was just a foot away from her. Slowly-calmly walking towards her to carry out my intentions.

'Aarush….', I heard a scream from upstairs. It was Aarush's mother. She came running towards him screaming his name in the hope that he might respond but I stabbed him numerous times. It was nowhere near possible for him to even move on his own.

I lost the hold of the knife, seeing her struggling for her son and I ran away with all the blood and tears on my clothes towards my home.

I got arrested that evening for attempt to murder. I lost everything in that moment of rage.

Saddest or the happiest part I don't know what to call it…
Aarush was safe, Aakriti and his mother managed to save
him and at that point she realized what she could have lost
and what he is to her and she saved him with all the
knowledge she had and after he recovered they both got
married.

They could have hated me for what I did or they could
have loved me for being the cupid of their life but I would
never find this out. I don't know where they went after all
this. I'm here in the prison, struggling with the fact that I
lost what I had or at least what I could have had but my
reality today is far more different than what I planned for
my life and I'm glad that they choose to get far from my
site because I don't know from where this rage came
suddenly and how I became someone who could stab a
person multiple times.. Not just a person but the man I
love but now all I know is next time the rage could be
more, the strength would be more and the desire for
revenge would be more.